The Ox of the
Wonderful Horns
and Other
African Folktales

Retold and illustrated by

Ashley Bryan

The Ox of the
Wonderful Horns
and Other
African Folktales

Atheneum   1993   New York

Maxwell Macmillan Canada
Toronto
Maxwell Macmillan International
New York   Oxford   Singapore   Sydney

"Elephant and Frog Go Courting" and "Frog and His Two Wives" are based on two stories found in Heli Chatelain's *Folktales of Angola,* Boston, 1894.

"The Ox of the Wonderful Horns" is based on a story found in George McCall's *Kaffir Folklore,* London, 1882.

"Ananse the Spider in Search of a Fool" is based on a story found in R. S. Rattray's *Akan-Ashanti Folktales,* Oxford, 1930.

"Tortoise, Hare and the Sweet Potatoes" is based on a story found in Henri Junod's *The Life of a South African Tribe,* volume 2, London, 1913.

Atheneum
Macmillan Publishing Company
866 Third Avenue
New York, NY 10022

Maxwell Macmillan Canada, Inc.
1200 Eglinton Avenue East
Suite 200
Don Mills, Ontario M3C 3N1

Macmillan Publishing Company is part of the Maxwell Communication Group of Companies.

First published 1971; reissued 1993
Printed in the United States of America
10 9 8 7 6 5 4 3 2 1
The text of this book is set in ITC Bookman Light.

Library of Congress Catalog Number 75-154749
ISBN 0-689-31799-9

For the brothers and sisters:
Charlie, Vanessa, Ashley,
Valerie, Denise. One each!

Contents

Ananse The Spider
in Search of a Fool

W e do not mean, we do not really mean, that what we
are going to say is true.

Hear my account of Spider Ananse and the fish traps.

Spider Ananse once lived by the sea. There were plenty
of fish in those waters. Yes, there were fish to be caught for
those who had traps made and set. But Ananse was not one
to be working like that.

"I'd like to catch and sell fish," he thought, "the regular
type and the shellfish, too. But if I'm to do that, I must hire
a fool to make, set, and pull the traps."

Spider was sure he'd have no trouble finding a fool. Once
he did, he planned to make great catches of fish, which he'd
sell in the market for cash. He would keep all the money
for himself and grow rich in the fish business.

"I'll pay the fool a few regular fish and maybe even some

shellfish," he told himself. "But as for money, of course, the fool will get none!"

So Spider Ananse set out to find a fool. He walked about the fishing village, calling, "I want a fool. I want a fool."

He saw a woman cooking. "I am looking for a fool," he said.

"A fool," she said, mocking him and shaking her wooden spoon. Spider ran off to the shore, where on the beach, he saw a busy fisherman.

"I am looking for a fool," said Spider.

"A pool?" asked the fisherman.

"No! A fool," said Spider.

"A tool?" asked the fisherman.

"A fool, a fool," howled Spider as he hurried off. "A fool indeed," he muttered, "but deaf."

And everywhere Ananse looked it was the same. No one listened to him. Nowhere could a fool be found.

After a long time, Ananse met Osana the Hawk. This time Ananse began in a new way. "Come," he said, "let's go and set fish traps."

But Osana had heard that Ananse was hunting a fool to go fishing, so he said, "Oh, I have no need to set fish traps. I have plenty of meat to eat."

Later Ananse met Anene the Crow. "Let us go and set fish traps," Ananse said.

"Why not?" said Crow. "I'll go with you."

"Wait here," said Spider Ananse, almost bursting with joy. "I won't be long." He ran home to get his knife.

While Ananse was gone, Anene the Crow rested in the shade of a silk-cotton tree. And when Hawk was sure that Spider was gone, he flew down.

"Watch out for Ananse," Osana warned. "Don't go with

him on this fish trap-setting trip. He's looking for a fool. He wants someone else to do the work. But he plans to sell all the regular fish, and the shellfish as well, and keep all the cash from the catch for himself."

"*Bakoo!*" said Anene the Crow. "I did not know. But now I do. Thank you Osana. Don't say any more. I will go with Ananse, and we shall see who does the work and who gets the money."

Spider Ananse soon returned with his knife. He and Crow set out at once for the bush to cut palm branches for traps.

When they came to a palm tree, Crow said to Spider, "Ananse, give me the knife. I will go cut the branches. You can sit here and take the weariness of my hard work."

Spider replied, "Anene, do you take me for a fool? No! I will do the cutting. You will sit aside and take the weariness of my work."

So Ananse the Spider did all of the cutting, while Anene the Crow sat aside sighing and yawning in weariness.

When Ananse had finished cutting the palms, Anene helped him tie them into a neat bundle.

Then Crow said, "Ananse, let me carry the bundle. You can trek after me and take the aches and pains of this back-breaking work."

"Oh, no," said Spider. "You must take me for a fool! Here! You help steady the load on my head. I will carry, and you can take the aches."

So Crow followed sighing and yawning and groaning beautifully, every step of the way. And Ananse carried.

When they reached Spider's hut, Crow helped Spider set the load on the ground.

"Now let me make the fish traps," said Crow. "Yes, let

me. I'll show you how. You can take the fatigue of my labors."

Spider replied, "Anene, never! Everyone knows that I'm a great weaver. Leave the trap making to me. You take the fatigue."

Crow chose the most comfortable mat in Spider's hut and stretched out on his back. There he lay, sighing and yawning and groaning and bawling, more woefully than ever.

"Fool," said Spider. "Have you no sense? Just listen to your moaning. It sounds as if you were dying."

Spider Ananse began to spin. He spun and he wove and he made palm mesh for the fish traps. He worked till they were well made and ready to be set.

"Let me carry the fish traps to the water," said Crow. "It's your turn to take the tiredness of all this trap making."

Spider said, "No, no, Anene! None of your tricks. I'll take the traps, and you can take the tiredness of the task."

They set out for the shore. Spider walked carefully, balancing the traps. Crow staggered behind sighing and yawning and groaning and bawling all the way.

At the beach, Crow said, "Father Spider, a beast lives in the sea. Let me stand in the water and set the fish traps. If the beast should bite me, then you can take the death."

Spider said, "Anene, I swear that that is not a bit fair. I shall set the traps. If the beast bites me, then you shall die."

So Spider Ananse toiled in the sea, setting the fish traps. No beast bit. And Anene watched comfortably. Then the two returned to Spider's hut and slept.

The next morning they arose at dawn and hurried down to the sea. They opened the traps and found two fish as their catch.

Crow said, "Ananse, these two fish are for you. Tomorrow, when the traps have caught four, it will be my turn to take them."

Spider exclaimed, "What a cheat you are! Do you take me for a fool? No sir! These two are yours. Tomorrow, I'll take the four."

Anene the Crow took the fish and cooked them. He made a fine dish of fufu and fish and ate it all himself.

The next day Spider and Crow examined the traps and found four fish.

Crow said, "Ananse, these four fish are yours. I'll take the next batch, whatever the catch. With this bait, we're bound to get eight."

Spider said, "I'm no fool! I withdraw my claim to these four. You take these and tomorrow I'll have the eight."

Crow took the fish and fried the four. He made a fine dish of fufu and fried fish and ate it all himself.

The next day when they inspected the traps, Spider counted eight fish as their catch.

"Take them, Ananse," said Crow. "I'll go back to the hut and wait for tomorrow's catch of sixteen."

Spider said, "I am no fool, Anene. You take the eight fish. I'll have tomorrow's sixteen."

Crow took the fish and baked the eight. He made a fine dish of fufu and baked fish and ate it all himself.

The next morning sixteen fish were caught in the traps. And by now the fish traps were well worn out.

Anene the Crow said, "Ananse, these fish traps are rotten. They will not catch fish any longer. But each trap will fetch a price in the marketplace. You take the sixteen fish and give me the rotten fish traps to sell."

"Oh, no!" said Spider. "You take the fish and sell them if

you can. I shall sell the rotten fish traps and keep the cash."

Crow picked up the sixteen fish, and Spider picked up his rotten fish traps. Together they went to the nearby village market.

A crowd soon surrounded Crow. People bargained and bid and bought his fish. In no time at all he had sold the sixteen. If he had had more, he would have sold more. But he did well, just the same, for he had a great mound of gold dust in his feathered purse.

When the crowd broke up, Spider Ananse still sat with his unsold traps.

Crow said to him, "Don't just sit there with your wares. Take up those perfectly rotten fish traps and let people discover that you have them. Walk around and talk about your treasured traps. Cry out! Let the villagers hear your voice. Make a loud noise. Don't think you can sell by sitting in silence."

Crow's fiery speech so inspired Spider that he leaped to his feet, lifted his traps, and sang out in a burst of pride and enthusiasm:

"Rotten fish traps for sale
Rare, bedraggled, and old
Treat your son and yourself
Pay in cowries or gold."

The village chief was astonished to hear such a ridiculous cry from the market place. Never before had his people been so insulted by a stranger.

"But where does this fellow come from?" he asked. "Send him to me!"

Spider Ananse went quickly at the call, calculating a sale

in cowries and gold. He was still busy making these calculations when the chief thundered:

"Do you suppose this is a village of fools?"

Spider trembled.

"Your friend Crow came and sold fine fish for a good profit. Did you sit by and not take notice? Then why do you seek to dispose of your useless, rotten fish traps among us?"

The chief was so angry that he called his men and said, "Flog him!"

Spider Ananse tried to flee, but he tripped over the loose palm strips of his rotten fish traps. As he flailed about to free himself, he became more entangled in the mesh until he was caught like a fish in his own fish traps.

As the blows drummed on Spider's back, he cried, *"Pui-pui, pui-pui!* Why do they beat p-po-poor me?"

Tears of pain flowed from Ananse's eyes. Then suddenly they became tears of shame. For, at last, Spider Ananse realized that when one seeks to make a fool of another, he is bound to make a bigger fool of himself.

This is my story. Whether it be bitter or whether it be sweet, take some of it elsewhere and let the rest come back to me.

Frog and
His Two Wives

Listen, let me tell the story of Frog Kumbuto who married two wives.

"*Kuo-kua*," he sang for one wife.

"*Kua-kuo*," he sang for the other.

He sprang high into the air. *Whish!* Twirling both legs, he whirled himself about and came down. *Whump!* He jumped again into the skies. *Whee!* It was a wonder to have two wives.

Frog Kumbuto built each wife a good house of her own on his land.

The first wife chose the sycamore grove on the east of his land. There he built her house. *Bam!*

The second wife chose the palm grove on the west of Frog's land. There he built her house. *Bohm!*

The middle ground was where Frog liked to be. Berry

bushes grew there with berries that Frog liked to lick, nibble, and bite for breakfast. And there was, as well, a tall nut tree for noonday shade and nuts; and nearby there lay a small rush marsh for an evening splash and bath. It was in the middle that Frog built his house. *Bosh!*

Well, the first wife cooked one meal for Frog each day. And the second wife cooked the other meal. The east house wife cooked for Frog as the sun rose in the east. The west house wife cooked for Frog as the sun set in the west. It was a fine plan. Frog swelled with pride when he saw how well it worked.

The sun shone day after day. And day after day for many months Frog ate at morning in the east and at evening in the west. But then the rainy season began.

Frog Kumbuto loved the rain. He sauntered about in delight. But by the thirteenth day of the rainy spell, Frog's two wives had become confused about the time of day. So it happened that one gray day, without knowing whether they were coming or going, the wives mixed up the mealtime plan. Well! Both began to cook for Frog at the same time.

Each wife fanned her fire and stirred her pot. Frog Kumbuto, not thinking about it, lay on his rush mat and smelled the delicious odor of juicy mush from the east and the aroma of lush spicy mush from the west. *Haah!*

In time the mush was cooked. Both wives looked up to see if Frog was coming. But Frog had not moved. What!

The first wife called her little son and said, "Hop now and fetch your father!"

The second wife said to her small daughter, "Rush now and fetch your father!"

Both children left quickly to fetch Father Frog. Skip-

ping and jumping and hopping from east and from west, they arrived at the same spot at the same time. *Thump!* They fell down on the rush mat beside Frog Kumbuto.

Regaining their feet and their breath, each child pulled one of Frog's arms as they sang out together, "Father come with me! Come with me! It's time to eat."

Now Frog was in a fix. He was pulled to the east. He was pulled to the west. Woe! He freed his arms and beat his breast.

"Oh, no!" he groaned as he spun around. He clutched his stomach. He pounded the ground.

"Both wives are calling, 'Come! Come! Come!' They are two, and I am one. If I go east to eat first, the west wife will pester me. 'Aha,' she'll say, 'so east wife is your chief wife, eh?' If I decide to feast with the west wife first, then the east wife will cry, 'Aho, Kumbuto! From the start I thought the west wife was your best beloved!'"

Frog sat down and wailed. He was so upset that he garbled his words. His cracked bass voice called out:

"Rye bam in bubble! I tam tin tubble!" Till finally he croaked it right: "I am in trouble!"

Now friends, the story is as I have told it. Plucky Frog Kumbuto married two wives. All went well until the day that both called him to mush at once. To this day he does not know what to do.

He sits in the marsh and cries:

"Kuo-kua! Kua-Kuo!"

It sounds funny, I know. Some people joke and say:

"Listen, Frog is croaking!"

But no! Frog is speaking. He is saying:

"I am in trouble!"

Pity poor Frog.

Elephant and Frog Go Courting

I never tire of telling the tale of Mr. Elephant and Mr. Frog who were courting the girls at the same house.

Frog and Elephant were enormously popular with the girls at that house. They were thoughtful and generous and always brought presents of flowers or fruit when they visited.

Indeed, everyone who knew Elephant and Frog agreed that, despite obvious differences, the two had much in common.

They were both very handsome, each in his own way, of course. They both loved the water, and both relished a walk through the forest, especially when the path led to the pretty girls' house. And although they were not the same size, they were the same age.

But why go on listing ways in which Frog and Elephant

were alike? There are so many and that's hardly the story. So let's go on.

It happened that one afternoon Frog visited the girls alone. He sat with them near the house in the shade of a silk-cotton tree, and they all sipped cool coconut milk.

The girls surrounded Frog and laughed at his witty talk. His conversation was more charming and clever than ever. He felt he was king of the forest! So when Elephant's sweetheart began to speak with great eloquence of Elephant's grace and elegance, at once Frog became angry.

He puffed himself up as large as he dared. He swelled with importance and said to her, "You know, of course, that Mr. Elephant is my horse."

"Is that true? Is that true?" the girls chorused. They were so excited that they danced around Frog. Well, now, Frog felt big, bigger even than Mr. Elephant. And when he left he hopped off into the forest as if he owned it all.

Elephant came to visit that night. As they saw him coming through the forest, the girls said to his sweetheart, "Look! Here comes Mr. Frog's horse!"

Elephant's sweetheart ran out to meet him. He gave her a basket of wild cherries, a bouquet of wild flowers, a tame hug, and a shy kiss.

The girl, however, hardly thanked Elephant at all for this. She was so full of Frog's remark that she simply blurted out, "We heard today from Mr. Frog that you are his horse."

"Better that than the other way round," quipped Elephant, and he laughed uproariously. The girls laughed, too, but then they repeated what Frog had said. They obviously believed it.

"Now wait a m-minute," stammered Elephant. "Me?

M-m-me? Mr. Frog's horse?"

"That's what he said."

"Ridiculous! He was k-k-kidding of course!"

"Oh, no," said Elephant's sweetheart. "He swore to us that he was serious."

Elephant was furious. He fumed and trumpeted and left in a rage. Behind him, he could hear the girls laughing as he went. He felt small, even smaller than Mr. Frog.

The next day Elephant went in search of Frog. He looked everywhere and finally caught him frisking in the river.

"Hello, Grandfather," Frog called affectionately. "Want to race?"

Elephant could not bring himself to say so much as one word. He simply reached out with his trunk and snatched Mr. Frog out of the water. He set his startled friend down *plop!* on a grass patch.

"Now look here, Grandson," he said still shaking with anger but at least not stammering. "Did you tell the girls that I was your horse?"

"What's that?" croaked Frog hopping up and down. "What? What? Easy there, Grandfather." Frog balled up his fists and advanced on Elephant menacingly. "Nobody accuses me of anything like that!"

"Calm down, Grandson," said Elephant backing away. He was impressed by Frog's display of anger and innocence. "It was my sweetheart. She said you swore I was your horse!"

"Now that's crazy!" Frog spluttered. "Come along, Grandfather! We'll find those girls and settle this foolishness right this minute."

Frog started out ahead of Elephant, but he soon fell far behind. Elephant was anxious to reach the girls, but he wanted to arrive with Frog. So he sat and waited. "Hurry up, Grandson," he called.

Frog caught up at last, huffing and puffing, and limping besides. "Oh, oh what a trail!" he whined. "I must have stepped on a thorn. My poor foot's sore. I can't keep up with you at all. I'll have to go home and tend to my foot."

"What?" trumpeted Elephant. "You can't turn back now, Grandson! Listen, the girls will take care of your foot once we get that remark settled. Hop up on my back. That way we'll arrive together. It won't take long."

"Thanks, Grandfather, but I really don't want to be a burden!"

"Oh, be quiet, Grandson! Don't be silly!"

So Frog hopped up on Elephant's back.

Elephant's back was broad, and the ride was smooth. Nevertheless Frog flopped about, flailing hands and feet as if he were about to fall off.

"Grandfather! Grandfather!" he soon shouted into Elephant's ear. "I'll have more than a hurt foot by the time we arrive if I don't get some reins to steady myself up here!"

Elephant stopped and stooped, and Frog limped off. Elephant wanted Frog to be quick about getting the reins, so he helped Frog pull long tendrills from a tall banyan tree.

Frog plaited the tendrils into a strong string, which he bound across Elephant's mouth. Then he limped back into place.

"Well, Grandfather! What a difference!" Frog exclaimed as he directed Elephant with the reins.

They went on steadily.

Suddenly Frog started whirling his arms as if he'd lost his mind. "My word, Grandfather!" he shouted. "We must have hit a cloud of flies and mosquitoes! I haven't seen this

many in all my born days. Do stop! I'd better get me a green-twig switch to flick off these rascal insects. Otherwise we'll be eaten alive before we arrive!"

Once more Elephant stopped and stooped. Frog limped down and moved slowly to a bush. He broke off a neat twig switch and twirled it gently as he returned to his place on Elephant's back.

Frog swished the twig-whip in great arcs and held the reins slack until they reached the edge of the forest. Just ahead, by the silk-cotton tree, was the house of the girls.

"Quick, Grandson," Elephant called. "Hop down. We are almost there."

Frog pretended not to hear. Instead he tightened the reins, pinching the tenderest tissues of Elephant's mouth. Elephant reared up in pain then plunged ahead. But Frog held on.

The girls heard the commotion and came to their door just as Elephant, with Frog astride, went racing by. Frog

was holding the reins smartly with one hand and whirling the twig whip with the other.

When they were well past the house, Frog jerked the left rein sharply and Elephant spun around. As they galloped back, the girls applauded. Really, they had never seen a more dramatic display of horsemanship.

Elephant sped with Frog into the forest along the same path they had come from in the first place. As soon as Frog knew the girls could no longer see them, he let go of the reins and flipped himself into the overhanging branches of the tree.

"Thanks for the ride, Grandfather horse," Frog croaked. And he hopped off quickly until he was lost among the leaves.

Elephant buffeted and butted and battered the trees. Bananas fell. Coconuts fell. Mangoes and figs fell. But no Frog fell.

Finally Elephant gave up. All the way home the birds sang, but that did not cheer him up at all. For in his mind he could only hear the girls saying, "So it's true. It's true indeed. Mr. Elephant is the horse of Mr. Frog."

There! I have told my tale of Elephant and Frog. Whether good, whether bad, there is nothing to add. I have finished.

Tortoise, Hare,
and the Sweet Potatoes

L isten, brothers and sisters, to this story of how Tortoise
outwitted Hare.

Hare was a born trickster. He was always dreaming up
new riddles and tricks to try on others. He'd spring an im-
possible riddle, wait a little, then rattle off the answer. Riddles and tricks, Hare never tired of either.

Tortoise on the other hand was much too busy keeping
her little pond clean to worry about tricking anyone. Animals came from field and forest, far and near, to drink in
the pond where she lived.

Tortoise believed in the proverb, "Give the passing trav-
eller water and you will drink news yourself." So, although
she rarely left her pool, her visitors kept her well informed.
She knew more than most and was seldom fooled.

It happened one season then that the news Tortoise

heard again and again was disgracefully bad. Someone was stealing, stealing food from all the fields around. Now most creatures were willing to give when another was hungry. But stealing was taboo.

Everyone asked, "Who would do what's taboo?" And no one knew. But Tortoise had a few well-founded ideas.

One day Hare came by Tortoise's pond. He drank his fill, then was ready for mischief. "Aha! Now to muddy the pond and have a little fun," he thought. He had never cared for the proverb, "Do not fill up the well after having drunk. Where would you drink tomorrow?"

Tortoise was on her guard, however, and all Hare could do was sit beside her and ask riddles. Tortoise answered every one.

"I know one you can't answer," said Hare. "Tell me the thing that you can beat without leaving a scar?"

"I live by it and I drink it," said Tortoise. "Water."

So Hare gave up trying to catch Tortoise with riddles. But he was not through.

After a while he said, "Now old Tortoise, let's go and till a field together."

"Me! Till the land? I can just manage to scratch out my little garden patch. How could I hoe a whole field with my short legs?"

"Short legs? Your legs are beautiful. Just the right length for hoeing."

"Do say! But how could I hold a hoe?"

"No problem at all. I'll tie you to it. I'd love to do that for you."

There was truth in that statement, Tortoise decided. Hare knew how to trick people, all right. But she wasn't taken in. She said aloud, "I don't think I'll try, thanks."

So they sat in silence. And after a while Hare said, "I'm hungry, Sis. Aren't you?"

"A little, but I don't have a leaf left in my garden."

"Well, poor thing, let me help you. I came upon a wide field of good things on my way here. Come on! Let's help ourselves to some of Wild Boar's sweet potatoes."

"Ooo, ooo! What are you saying? You know better than that, Mr. Hare. No pilfering!"

So they sat on in silence, Hare not willing to give up.

And after a while Tortoise became really hungry. Besides she had a few worthwhile ideas.

"Where did you say that field of sweet potatoes was?" she asked.

"It's not far, just past the bush."

"Well now, said Tortoise, seeming to overcome her scruples, "I guess Wild Boar won't miss a few."

Off they went together. And when they came to Wild Boar's field it was no job at all to root out the sweet potatoes. Soon Hare's sack was filled.

Hare with a great show of strength steadied the bag on Tortoise's back, and they headed for the bush to cook the potatoes. When they found a good quiet spot, they gathered dry grass and made a crackling fire in which the sweet potatoes were soon roasted.

"Mmm-yum," said Tortoise as she bit into one.

"Wait a minute," said Hare. "Did you hear that?"

"Mmm-yum," said Tortoise, her mouth full of sweet potato.

"Stop munching and mumbling!" said Hare. "What if we're caught?"

"Mmm-um-yum," said Tortoise, reaching for another sweet potato.

"Wow-wow," said Hare, "do you want to be beaten and bitten by Wild Boar? Put down that potato! We've got to scout around first and make sure that Boar's not after us."

Hare forced Tortoise to stop eating, and they went off in opposite directions to scout the field.

Tortoise who had a good notion of what was afoot and was ready, waddled a few reluctant steps; Hare bounded out of sight. As soon as he was gone, Tortoise turned back, took another sweet potato, and crawled into the empty sack.

"Mmm-yum," she said. She was about to crawl out for another when suddenly a rain of roasted sweet potatoes fell around her. Hare was back, very quietly, very quickly.

"Good," said Tortoise, biting into another sweet potato, "saves me the trouble."

Old trickster Hare filled his sack in a hurry.

"Mistress Tortoise," he shouted then. "Get going! Take off! Run for your life! Wild Boar and his big, fat wife are coming."

He threw the bag over his back. "Save yourself! Fly!" he cried, but inside he thought: "Best trick in ages. Now to put some miles between me and Slowpoke." He took off, running and laughing as hard as he could.

Tortoise made herself comfortable in the sack. She ate one sweet potato after another. "Too bad Hare is missing the feast," she thought. "But maybe he prefers running to eating."

Hare ran as fast and as far as he could. By the time he stopped to rest, Tortoise had eaten all of the finest and fattest sweet potatoes. In fact, there was only one very small sweet potato left.

"Aha good," said Hare as he put his hand into the sack. "Too bad Tortoise is miles away."

"Sweet potatoes," Hare sang, "sweet, sw-eeeet potatoes!" Tortoise put the last sweet potato into Hare's outstretched hand.

When Hare saw the size of it, he cried, "Ha! What a miserable one this is. I didn't run my head off for that!" And he flung it into the bushes.

Hare put his hand back into the sack. This time he felt a big one, a nice firm, juicy one.

"Oho!" he chortled, "here's a beauty. What a prize!"

Imagine Hare's surprise when he saw what he had in his hand.

"Mistress Tortoise!" he cried as he dropped her to the ground.

Hare shook out the sack. Tears of unbelief welled up in his eyes when he saw it was empty. "My potatoes, the sweet ones I rooted up . . . oh no, oh no! You didn't eat mine, too? Sister Tortoise, how could you be so unfair?"

But Mistress Tortoise didn't stand around for the lecture. She took to her toes and scuttled away to her pond as fast as she could go.

Hungry Hare lay on the ground and screeched, "Woe, woe, that wily Mistress Tortoise ate all my sweet potatoes. Wa, Waa. How awful of her. When I think that I carried her all the while, I could cry!"

And that's just what he did.

The Ox of the Wonderful Horns

There are those who enjoy telling of the boy who made his fortune with nothing but a pair of ox horns.

Mungalo, that was the boy's name, and he was the son of a wealthy chief. His father had many wives. They loved their husband, but they were jealous of Mungalo's mother. She was the first and favorite wife. They dared not offend her, but they found ways to worry Mungalo. They found ways to be cruel to him.

But each day when Mungalo went out with the sheep and the goats, he tapped the sparrow drum he always took with him. The sound of the little drum made him forget how badly he was treated by his father's wives.

Each wife did her best to outshout the rest when Mungalo returned in the evening with the animals. Just as his head cleared the crest of the hill near the kraal, he'd hear their calls:

"Mungalo! Mungalo! Mungalo!"

Each wife always had a job for him to do—at once! Mungalo did all he could as fast as he could, but nothing ever pleased his hard-hearted mothers.

It was as the proverb says: "They gave him a basket to carry water."

Only his own mother was loving and gave him toys and kindness and words of comfort. But, alas, Mungalo was still a child when she died. The toys she had given him, especially some little clay oxen that she had made, broke one by one, until he had none left. But he kept whole in his heart his mother's promise that when he was old enough his father would give him a great white ox.

The years passed. Each day at dawn Mungalo set out to find a good grazing place for the sheep and the goats. While he worked, his brothers, the sons of many mothers, played. When he came home, he found no welcome but more work. Yet Mungalo suffered his mistreatment in silence and said nothing to his father.

After his initiation into the tribe, Munaglo's father gave him a great white ox, just as his mother had promised. It was a beautiful beast with wonderful horns, the finest of all of his father's cattle.

Mungalo thought that then he would be treated with respect. He was old enough to herd the great oxen, and he owned the most admired ox of all.

But the jealousy of his mean mothers only inspired them to find more ways of making Mungalo unhappy. So he decided he must leave home.

One morning, he mounted the great white ox and journeyed until he had left the land of his father far behind.

For seven days and seven nights the boy and the ox

travelled on. They stopped only to rest and to eat the food of the lands they traversed.

Toward noon on the eighth day, they crossed a wide plain. It was so hot that shimmering heat waves made the ground seem to heave and swell like an ocean.

Mungalo was hungry and thirsty. He looked about him. But nowhere on that dry plain did he see the least sign of plant or tree or water.

Mungalo stroked the ox gently and said, "Dear friend, I've led you from a land we knew to an unknown plain. I had hoped to escape the curse of my father's wives. But what could be worse than to die here of hunger and thirst?"

Moved by his friend's distress, the ox spoke:

> *"Mungalo, listen! At your command*
> *Food or clothes or house and land*
> *I can provide. Strike my horns.*
> *Three times the right, you'll have your wish*
> *Twice the left and all will vanish."*

Mungalo did as the ox bid. He struck the right horn three times. Suddenly cool grass covered the ground. On it were bowls of pungent food and luscious fruit.

Mungalo leaped from the ox's back and thanked his friend. Together they ate and drank and were refreshed.

Then Mungalo mounted the ox and struck the left horn twice. Immediately the remaining food was gone. It seemed to have vanished into the horn itself.

The two travelled on.

For seven days and seven nights Mungalo and the ox of the wonderful horns crossed the open plains. They stopped only to rest, to sleep, and to refresh themselves with the food struck from the horns of the great white ox.

At last they came to a virgin forest. Great trees and roots and vines like tangled ropes barred the way. But, at the touch of the ox's hooves, roots and vines moved aside. Tall ferns parted. Low leaves and branches lifted above Mungalo's head. The movement of the plants allowed thin beams of light to come in, and sun spots scattered and danced like balls of gold. The whole scene seemed enchanted to Mungalo.

Deep in the forest their path opened upon a clearing. There a herd of cattle grazed. At the head of the group stood a large bull.

Mungalo saw no way around the herd, and the leader challenged the route the white ox took. The bull tossed his head and pawed the ground as the travellers approached. The earth shook, and Mungalo trembled; but the ox spoke:

> *"Do not fear the might*
> *Of this fierce bull. We'll fight,*
> *And I will win. We've far*

To go until we are
Before the towering mountain wall
Where I will fight. Where I will fall."

During the battle Mungalo crouched at one edge of the clearing. The cattle lined the other side.

In the force and fury of the fight, torn grass rose from the ground and formed a dark green cloud around the ox and the bull. The sound of clashing horns and striking hooves drummed like a huge sparrow drum. The noise filled the clearing.

When the tumult stilled, the grass cloud settled and Mungalo saw the fierce bull dead. His ox of the wonderful horns came toward him.

Mungalo leaped lightly astride the ox and the herd parted. The two passed unharmed through the strange creatures and into the forest.

Seven days and seven nights Mungalo and the great white ox pushed on. They journeyed through dense jungles and deep ravines. They crossed hills and wide streams.

Finally they crossed a narrow stream and came upon carefully planted, fertile fields. It seemed strange to Mungalo that no one was laboring or gathering there.

Then he saw, looming ahead, a towering mountain. It rose like a huge wall. But some great force had, it seemed once moved the land beneath the mountain and had split the high stone wall. So now a narrow cleft led through the mountain to a village beyond.

Guarding the narrow pass was a huge bull, looking more fierce than the last beast the ox had battled. Nearby grazed a dun-colored herd of cattle.

Mungalo immediately recognized the place as the one

described by the ox. In sorrow he fell forward and lay still on the ox's back. Then, for some reason strengthened, he slid down, touched the wonderful horns, and rubbed the dear beast's forehead.

The ox spoke:

> *"Goodbye Mungalo. At your command*
> *Food or clothes or house and land*
> *My horns will give. When I am gone*
> *This power remains for you alone."*

In the battle that followed, Mungalo's ox of the wonderful horns was killed. When the dust cloud the fight had stirred up settled, the ox lay on the ground, and the bull and its herd had disappeared.

Mungalo severed the horns from the ox's head and bound them carefully to the belt at his waist. Tears filled his eyes. When they cleared, the ox had disappeared as completely as the bull and the cows.

Mungalo walked slowly through the cleft in the mountain and came out at the village beyond. There he saw the townspeople cooking a tough root. Mungalo soon learned that this weed was the only food left in the village. The mysterious herd had pounded through the village days before and had scattered the grain that had been stored.

When the villagers saw the direction from which Mungalo had come, they asked in surprise, "How did you get through the pass? A huge fierce bull has blocked the path for days."

Mungalo did not wish to tell the tale of the great white ox. He did not want anyone to know the secret of the magic horns, so he said, "No herd or huge fierce bull was there

when I went through. You are fools to feed upon roots when your fields are full of food."

The villagers rejoiced when they heard that the mountain pass was clear. Drumming began, and the people danced. The chief singer sang praise songs to the stranger for his good news. Now the people could return to their fields without fear.

The singer invited Mungalo into his hut for the night. Since they were both hungry, Mungalo secretly tapped the right horn. Three times he tapped it and food appeared before them.

The singer was astonished to see a sudden abundance of food before him. He ate heartily, determined all the while to learn the trick. He smiled and quickly poured more palm wine each time Mungalo emptied his gourd. But Mungalo's tongue did not trip and tell the secret.

At the end of the feast Mungalo tapped the left horn

twice, and the food was gone. Both men settled down to sleep.

But during the night the singer, who had only pretended to sleep, crept to Mungalo's side. He had guessed the secret, and now he untied the magic horns from Mungalo's belt, replacing them with two others. He hid the wonderful horns and lay down again.

In the morning the whole village rose early to go through the mountain pass to their fields. Mungalo thanked his host and started on his way. He was happy for he knew that his friend's spirit lived with him in the wonderful horns, and he sang as he went along.

Near noon the sun shone from straight overhead and Mungalo's shadow hid underfoot. He was hungry and tired, so he stopped to rest.

The first thing he did was to strike the right horn three times, but nothing happened. He tried again, but no food came from the horn. Then Mungalo knew that his wonderful horns had been exchanged for worthless ones.

There was nothing to do but go straight back to the hut in the village where he had spent the night. Once there, he heard the singer chanting praise songs as he tapped the horns. But no matter how exalted his praises to the color and curve of the horns, and no matter how skillfully he rapped them, nothing happened.

Finally, in a fury, he flung the horns into a far corner of the hut. In his rage, he rammed his head against the door so hard he burst through.

The villagers could not understand why the singer was so wild. They knew nothing of the magic horns. And now that they had returned from their fields, they were too busy cooking and eating their own good food to care.

Mungalo entered the hut, took the magic horns, and left the others. He knew now that the good of the wonderful horns could not fall into the hands of a thief. And he was glad.

As he travelled on, Mungalo sensed the spirit and power of the ox protecting him all along the way. He did not count how many times the sun rose and set upon his adventures. Each day he walked contented, seeing and hearing strange and wonderful things. Each night he slept beneath the stars believing that the ox's horns kept him from harm.

Mungalo paid little attention to himself. He was too busy marvelling at the wonders about him. He never never saw that his clothes were spotted and torn. He did not know that he was streaked with the dust of travel. Yet he longed now and then for a companion. So one night when he saw a house by a field, he decided to stop. He knocked at the door, and a man came.

The man looked at Mungalo, turned, and closed the door. He did not invite Mungalo in.

Mungalo could not understand this until the next day when he came to a stream and looked at himself in the still water. He scarcely recognized his own reflection. He laughed remembering the look on the man's face. No wonder he had been turned away!

Mungalo splashed and washed and swam until he was clean. Then he dried in the sun and wished for new clothes. He struck the horn as he spoke:

"I knocked at a door
I was chased as a thief.
Please dress me in clothes
Due the son of a chief."

Immediately an array of marvellous clothes and ornaments was displayed on the branches of low bushes. Mungalo dressed in the bright cloths he liked best. He chose well-wrought spiral silver pendants, bead ornaments and gold rings. He refastened his belt of horns and draped a gorgeous mantle over his shoulders. Then he entered the next village.

Here, Mungalo's royal appearance won for him a warm welcome. He was greeted by the chief of the village and invited to stay in his house. He was treated like a prince, and was served with grace and dignity by the chief's daughter.

The young girl's beauty filled Mungalo's eyes and heart. He gave rich cloths as gifts to the father, and he offered the daughter gold ornaments that glowed against her dark skin.

Three moons passed, and Mungalo shared more and

more in the life of the village. He helped the chief in his duties, and at night the villagers crowded around the fire to hear Mungalo tell tales from the land of his father.

Mungalo's love for the chief's daughter grew, and his acts of generosity and manliness soon won her heart.

After a time they were married. The food furnished by Mungalo's new family and the fine fare from the magic horns provided a feast that lasted for days. The drumming and dancing and singing did not stop until the last of the food had been eaten and the last pot of palm wine had been emptied.

A year later Mungalo returned with his wife to his father's village. The chief's wives prepared a lavish dinner to celebrate the son's return. They saw that their old evil ways had come to no good end. So they forgot their old jealousies and treated him well. They outdid each other in praise for Mungalo, his wife, and his wealth.

Mungalo and his wife settled on the ancestral lands

given him by his father. He wished on the magic horns for a house fit for the son of a chief. Later, as the family grew, he enlarged his fine dwelling by new wishes on the horns.

Mungalo told many tales of his adventures, but he never told the secret of the wonderful horns. Awake they were with him. Asleep they were nearby.

So the spirit of the great white ox stayed close to Mungalo throughout his life. For even when he became the honored leader of the tribe it was said that he was never parted from those wonderful horns.